THIS EMPLOYEE HANDBOOK BELONGS TO:

_____

iNgen

EMPLOYEE HANDBOOK

ISLA NUBLAR

Costa Rica

Owen —
I'll probably hate myself for
this, but could you take a
look at our new employee
handbook? I'd love your
input on the asset and safety
sections in particular. Just
please try to keep the snarky
comments to a minimum.
   —C

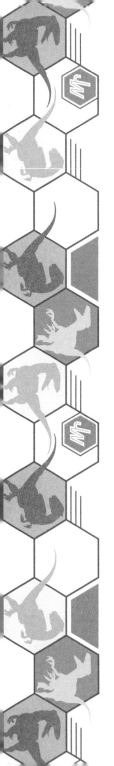

Claire,

I flagged a few spots I thought could use work. But tell you what—let's discuss it at Margaritaville. Whaddya say?

— Owen

WELCOME TO JURASSIC WORLD

from Operations Manager, Claire Dearing

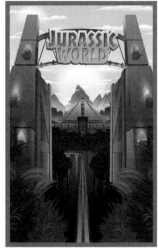

Welcome to Jurassic World, the most technologically-advanced and safest theme park in the world! As a member of our elite team, you will bring history to life for an average of 22,000 visitors a day. Our guests arrive on Isla Nublar expecting a heart-pounding adventure in a fun, clean, and, above all, safe environment. It is your job to help deliver that experience.

Your part begins with the information in this Employee Handbook. Learn it; study it; know it. Familiarize

yourself with all our facilities, attractions, and, most importantly, our assets— *the dinosaurs*. No matter what your job, we expect every Jurassic World employee to be part guide, part educator.

(continued)

(continued from previous page)

That means a geneticist or paleoveterinarian must be able to direct a visitor to the nearest restroom, and a cart vendor or shopkeeper must be prepared to explain the basics of DNA. And all employees must know our safety protocols backward and forward. Read this handbook and be prepared to discuss it at your upcoming orientation. At that time, you can turn in your paperwork, receive your housing assignment, and ask any questions you might have.

Finally, on behalf of Simon Masrani, our board of directors, and myself, welcome to Jurassic World! Today marks the first step on a journey into the past and a path to a bright future.

Claire Dearing

Claire Dearing

Claire

I'd loosen up just a bit here. Try to make it more personal. Maybe tell them about your internship. Give them hope. I mean, if you could work your way up the ladder anyone can!

SECTION 1: INTRODUCTION 6

SECTION 2: THE ATTRACTIONS 9

SECTION 3: MEET THE ASSETS.. 17

SECTION 4: JURASSIC WORLD EMPLOYMENT POSITIONS............................ 33

SECTION 5: EMPLOYEE RULES AND REGULATIONS 49

SECTION 6: EMPLOYEE PERKS AND BENEFITS 56

SECTION 7: SAFETY PROTOCOLS.. 65

SECTION 8: CAREER ADVANCEMENT/EDUCATIONAL DEVELOPMENT 74

SECTION 9: DINOSAUR GENETICS AND BIOLOGY... 81

SECTION 10: CLOSING COMMENTS / EMPLOYEE ACKNOWLEDGEMENT ...94

Employee sounds so
SUBSERVIENT.

Maybe something like
Team Member

is better?

A NOTE FROM JURASSIC WORLD'S OWNER AND CEO, SIMON MASRANI

In 1997, Dr. John Hammond entrusted me with his dying wish— create a theme park where visitors could come face-to-face with living, breathing dinosaurs! He insisted I spare no expense, and that's what I've done to create Jurassic World, the greatest theme park on earth!

The key to a happy life is to accept you are never actually in control.
Simon Masrani

Our mission is to ensure every guest has fun. In Jurassic World, fun means being thrilled! Visitors should remember our majestic creatures for the rest of their lives. And as a Jurassic World employee, it is your job to make that happen.

Finally, I hope that you also remain as amazed by the prehistoric wonders on Isla Nublar as I am. After all, Jurassic World exists to remind us how very small we are on this globe that began spinning through space millions of years before we ever came along.

Simon Masrani

Simon Masrani

WOW.
Our visitors-per-day average
is under capacity? Must keep you up at
night, Claire :)

JURASSIC WORLD STATISTICS

Park capacity	**30,000 VISITORS**
Average # of visitors per day	**22,000**
# of dinosaur species	**20 (14 HERBIVORES AND 6 CARNIVORES)**
Amount of food consumed each week	**15 TONS**
# of gallons of water in Mosasaurus Lagoon	**3 MILLION**
# of restaurants and cafes	**15**
# of visitors to Jurassic World the first year	**8 MILLION, FROM 90 COUNTRIES**
# of volts in Mosasaurus Stadium electric fence	**10,000**

If only folks knew how many
dinosaurs there actually are
on this island...

= 15 TONS

! DANGER i
HIGH VOLTAGE
10,000 VOLTS
JURASSIC WORLD

MUST-KNOW FACTS

JURASSIC WORLD

- Park hours are 8 a.m. to 10 p.m.
- Jurassic World consists of the Theme Park, Resort, and the Hammond Creation Lab.

- A minimum of 20 attractions operate at any time.
- The park is divided into 6 sectors. **Sector 5 is restricted: authorized personnel only!**
- Main Street features 26 shops and 12 restaurants/cafes
- Jurassic World is ADA accessible

ISLA NUBLAR

- 120 miles off the west coast of Costa Rica in Central America
- 8 miles long and 3 miles wide at the widest point
- A total of 22 square miles
- Average annual temperature is 75 °F
- Ecology: Tropical

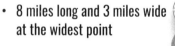

KNOW YOUR THEME PARK

To ensure a seamless experience for our guests, employees should familiarize themselves with all of our attractions.

MONORAIL

This is the main artery of Jurassic World. Our air-conditioned transportation system picks up arriving guests at Ferry Landing, passes through the famous Jurassic World Gate, and arrives at Main Street where guests find shops, restaurants, and our state-of-the art Innovation Center. From there, the monorail can take them to every attraction, or they can ride the loop for an overview of the park. *Monorail departs every 20 minutes.*

MONORAIL STATIONS

- Ferry Landing
- Main Street/Innovation Center
- Petting Zoo
- Egg Spinner
- Gyrosphere Valley
- Gondola Lift

- Cretaceous Cruise
- The Aviary
- Gallimimus Valley
- Triceratops Territory
- Hotel Complex
- Botanical Gardens

INNOVATION CENTER

This 20,000 square ft. "temple" to the spirit of innovation is where technology meets prehistory. Built in 2005, our dazzling welcome center features guided tours and more than 100 interactive exhibits, including Digging for Dinosaurs; the Holoscape, featuring life-size holograms of the assets; and the *Mr. DNA* show, a fun introduction to genetics, "the building blocks of life."

The Center is also home to the world-famous Hammond Creation Lab for asset development. Here, two to five new assets are cloned, incubated, and hatched each week through the magic of genetic engineering. Visitors cannot enter the lab, but can get a great view from the observation area.

Our world-class Control Center is also housed in the Innovation Center, but is also off-limits to guests. It is manned 24/7 by expert technicians, who monitor assets via tracking implants, engage our no-fail invisible fence, and oversee all park safety and security.

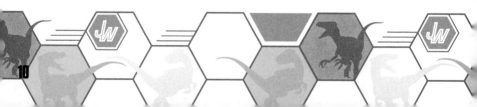

GYROSPHERE

Ball bearings are the secret to the gyro-rolling action in these gravity-defying pods, which always remain upright. A joystick puts drivers in control as they glide past 30 species of dinosaurs, including *Apatosaurus*, *Parasaurolophus*, *Stegosaurus*, and *Triceratops*. Pods travel at 5 m.p.h., outpacing the fastest Apatosaurus by 2 miles. All the assets in Gyrosphere Valley are relatively docile, but they should never be underestimated!

AVIARY

Jurassic World's enormous, glassed-in sanctuary is home to Pteranodons and Dimorphodons, the only living dinosaurs that fly. This high-security structure, built in 2004, was designed to exceed safety standards. The Aviary features indoor pools stocked with fish, as well as nests and thermal air currents that let these soaring predators coast on outstretched wings

CRETACEOUS CRUISE

Guests kayak down the pristine Cretaceous River that runs along the west side of Isla Nublar as our veteran tour guides lead them past a lush tropical forest brimming with 100 species of prehistoric life. This attraction is for novices and veteran kayakers, but it's a workout, so they should be physically fit. *Visitors burn off an average of 500 calories on this trip.*

GENTLE GIANTS PETTING ZOO

This is a beloved attraction for children and adults alike. Guests are invited to pet, feed, and even hug our gentler baby dinosaurs. We provide saddles for *Baby Triceratops* rides. (Helmets required.) The average weight of these young herbivores is 800 lbs. Each one consumes an average of 24 lbs. of plants a day.

TYRANNOSAURUS REX KINGDOM

Our most impressive asset, our *T. rex* has lived on Isla Nublar for more than 25 years and is the most popular attraction in Jurassic World. Visitors flock here to catch her regular feedings, which happen every 2 hours, rain or shine. That's because she eats 308 lbs. of meat every day! Her favorite meal: goats. *This show may be disturbing for small children.*

(Read more about the T. rex in Section 3: Meet the Assets)

Mosasaurus Feeding Show/ Underwater Observatory

Patrons love to watch this fierce predator leap out of her tank and clamp her massive jaws around a whole Great White shark. When she crashes back into the pool, guests are soaked in a delightful gush of water. To add to the experience, an astonishing, one-of-a-kind hydraulic seating system lowers guests into an Underwater Observatory, where they can get a closer look at the *Mosasaurus* as she dives and consumes her prey. Ponchos are recommended, especially in front rows. *Not for young children.*

Ponchos (for sale in all our gift shops) are recommended.
Read more about the Mosasaurus in Section 3: Meet the Assets.

Former Game Warden of Jurassic Park, Robert Muldoon, discovers *Velociraptors* cooperate with each other when they attack.

1992

1993

Dr. John Hammond brings his grandchildren and experts to Isla Nublar for a pre-opening tour of Jurassic Park. Due to tragic mishaps, park never opens.

1994

Dr. Wu returns to Jurassic Park to help clean up and catalog dinosaurs.

InGen raids Isla Sorna to get dinosaurs for the once-planned Jurassic Park: San Diego. The mission fails when caged dinosaurs are released and go on a rampage. InGen survivors transport an adult *T. rex* to San Diego, but it escapes and wreaks havoc. Finally, it is captured and returned to Isla Sorna. Plans for Jurassic Park: San Diego scrapped.

1997

Paul and Amanda Kirby search for their missing son with hired soldiers and Dr. Alan Grant and his assistant, Billy Brennan. The Kirbys find their son, but the group lets the *Pteranodons* escape, causing several deaths. The U.S. Military rescues survivors.

2001

1998

Masrani Corporation acquires InGen. Simon Masrani plans Jurassic World with Dr. Wu's help.

1997

Simon Masrani meets with Dr. John Hammond to discuss acquiring InGen. Dr. Hammond dies later that year.

Vic Hoskins' team captures the *Pteranodons*. Masrani later hires Hoskins as a security expert at Jurassic World.

Dinosaurs are moved from Isla Sorna to Isla Nublar

2004

2002-2004

Masrani Corporation builds Jurassic World on Isla Nublar.

2005

Jurassic World opens on May 30th. More than 8 million visitors from 90 countries attend that year. Operations have continued to run smoothly and engage newcomers year after year...

JURASSIC PARK TIMELINE

InGen clones the first dinosaur—a *Triceratops*—on Isla Sorna, Costa Rica.

1986

1984

Dr. John Parker Hammond's company, InGen, begins cloning efforts using prehistoric DNA.

1988

Dr. John Hammond makes Dr. Henry Wu Chief Geneticist and starts building Jurassic Park on Isla Nublar. The same year, dinosaurs are moved to Jurassic Park.

VISITOR MAP

Guests receive
this park map in their
"Welcome to Jurassic World"
packet.

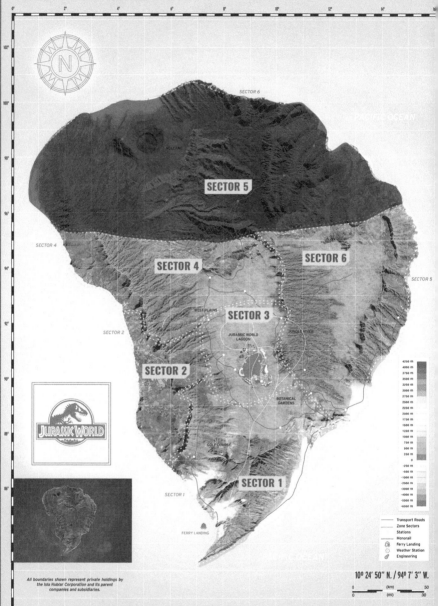

ISLA NUBLAR

SECTOR 6

PACIFIC OCEAN

SECTOR 5

VOLCANO

SECTOR 4

SECTOR 4

SECTOR 6

SECTOR 5

WESTPLAINS

SECTOR 3

SECTOR 2

JURASSIC WORLD LAGOON

JUNGLE RIVER

SECTOR 2

BOTANICAL GARDENS

JURASSIC WORLD

GOLF COURSE

SECTOR 1

SECTOR 1

FERRY LANDING

PACIFIC OCEAN

4250 m
4000 m
3750 m
3500 m
3250 m
3000 m
2750 m
2500 m
2250 m
2000 m
1750 m
1500 m
1250 m
1000 m
750 m
500 m
250 m
0
-250 m
-500 m
-1000 m
-2000 m
-3000 m
-4000 m
-5000 m
-6000 m

Transport Roads
Zone Sectors
Stations
Monorail
Ferry Landing
Weather Station
Engineering

10º 24' 50" N. / 94º 7' 3" W.

0   (km)   50
0   (mi)   30

ISLA NUBLAR

This Isla Nublar Map is for employees only. It marks all 6 sectors of the park, including Sector 5 at the north end of the island. *This sector is restricted. Authorized personnel only!*

ISLA NUBLAR

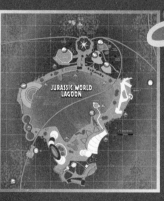

JURASSIC WORLD LAGOON

PLEASE NOTE:

Certain rides and attractions have restrictions. See details at ride entrance. Some may be too intense for young children.

Please abide by all safety warnings and instructions on posted signs throughout the Park. Proper attire - including shoes and shirts - must be worn at all times. We are eager to make your Isla Nublar Experience as fully exciting and memorable as possible. If you have any questions or concerns, please contact Guest Relations or speak with any one of our Isla Guides.

MONORAIL STATION

PARK HIGHLIGHTS

TRICERATOPS TERRITORY

T-REX KINGDOM

MOSASAURUS FEEDING SHOW

GALLIMIMUS VALLEY

CRETACEOUS CRUISE

PACHY ARENA

INNOVATION CENTER

CREATION LAB

UNDERWATER OBSERVATORY

THE AVIARY

THE EGG SPINNER

BAMBOO FOREST

GYROSPHERE

GOLF COURSE

BOTANICAL GARDENS

GENTLE GIANTS PETTING ZOO

WATER PARK

GONDOLA LIFT

TOURIST REGIONS

RIDES / ATTRACTIONS

DINOSAUR SHOWS

SCANNER KIOSKS

MONORAIL STATION

FERRY LANDING

HOTEL COMPLEX

DINING

INFORMATION

CHILD CARE

CALL CENTER

RESTROOM

MEDICAL

RECYCLING

PARK KEY

DINOSAURS

These prehistoric reptiles ruled the earth from about 245 million years ago to 66 million years ago. Scientists think an asteroid hit the earth, or some other destructive event wiped them out along with most life on the planet. But through state-of-the-art genetic engineering, our scientists have brought these magnificent creatures back to life.

Always remember that dinosaurs are Jurassic World's primary assets—why our visitors travel here from all over the world. So familiarize yourself with the information in this section and get to know some of the park's biggest celebrities.

DINOSAUR FACTS

"DINOSAUR"
comes from the Greek word *deinos*, meaning "terrible" and *sauros* meaning "lizard"

CLOSEST MODERN RELATIVE
birds

PALEONTOLOGIST
a scientist who studies dinosaurs

 # OF DINOSAUR SPECIES
about 700 (that we know of)

CONTINENTS ON WHICH DINOSAUR FOSSILS WERE FOUND
all 7, including Antarctica

EATING HABITS

Some are herbivores; they only eat plants. Others, like *T. rex* and *Carnotaurus*, are ferocious meat-eaters that devour their prey

TEETH

A dinosaur's teeth are continually replaced throughout its life

BRAIN SIZE

Human newborns have bigger brains than many adult dinosaurs. A grown *Stegosaurus*'s brain is the size of a walnut

TAILS

Some are more than 45 ft. long. They help dinosaurs balance when running

OUR MOST POPULAR DINOSAUR SPECIES

VELOCIRAPTOR

Pronounced: *vel-oss-ih-rap-tor*

Do not underestimate this asset. Her name means "swift thief" because she's fast and smart. Though this is a smaller dinosaur, the curved claws jutting from her back feet are used to pin down prey. That's when the *Velociraptor's* powerful jaws go to work. These dinosaurs have distinct personalities, but they're pack hunters that work in groups to herd prey into a kill zone.

Hey, Owen,
Any feedback on this?
Especially about your
pals, the Velociraptors?

—C

Here's one of my favorite pics of my "pal"

STATS

Length: 11 ft.
Weight: 130 lbs.
Diet: Carnivore; eats smaller dinosaurs and other animals

Interesting Fact:
This biped (two-footed) runs 40 mph; 50 when hungry.

Tyrannosaurus Rex (T. Rex)

Pronounced: *tie-ran-oh-sawr-us reks*

This colossal lizard's name means, "king tyrant lizard," a title certainly befitting the mostly highly-visited attraction in the park. But this female asset should actually be more appropriately hailed as the "Queen." Her bite is ten times that of an adult alligator—that's roughly 8,000 pounds of pressure!

STATS

Length: 40 ft.
Weight: 9 tons
Diet: Carnivore; eats smaller dinosaurs and other animals

Interesting Fact:
T. rex's ears are attuned to low-frequency sound.

My "pals" have names: Blue, Delta, Echo, and Charlie, and they're offlimits to visitors. Don't forget, this is InGen's side project, not an attraction. Tell our employees to send visitors to see other Raptors in the park.
Say something like: we are studying and training four remarkable Velociraptors and have learned that they bond with humans and even show signs of empathy.

STYGIMOLOCH (STIGGY)

Pronounced: *stig-ee-mo-lock*

This spiny dinosaur's name means River Styx Demon, but she is only somewhat aggressive. She's on the small side 200 pounds—the weight of some human beings. But unlike any of us, she eats 10-20 pounds of plant life every day.

STATS

Length: 7.2 ft.
Weight: 200 lbs.
Diet: Herbivore; eats ferns and low-lying soft plants

Interesting Fact:
Communicates primarily through snorts and grunts.

Make sure you add something about her thick skull and how she likes to headbutt the double-thick glass of her paddock

Oh. And she HATE it when you whistl

CARNOTAURUS

Pronounced: *car-no-tawr-us*

At 2.5 tons, this asset, whose name means "meat-eating bull," is considered a featherweight. But don't underestimate her. She's an aggressive creature that sizes up her prey before striking. Then she eats it fast, so *Tyrannosaurus* can't steal her meal—or make a meal of the *Carnotaurus* herself. Ancestors of this asset lived in Patagonia, South America.

STATS

Length: 34 ft.
Weight: 2.4 tons
Diet: Carnivore; small to medium creatures like turtles and smaller dinosaurs

Interesting Fact:
She makes low, rumbling calls similar to her alligator and crocodile cousins.

TRICERATOPS & BABY TRICERATOPS

Pronounced: *try-ser-a-tops*

A crowd favorite, the *Triceratops* is the second-most visited asset in the park next to the *T. rex*.

STATS

For ADULT
Length: 26 ft.
Weight: 10 tons
Diet: Herbivore; feeding on cycads, palms, and other tough plants

Interesting Fact:
Jaws are packed with teeth that act as huge scissors to slice through even the toughest plants.

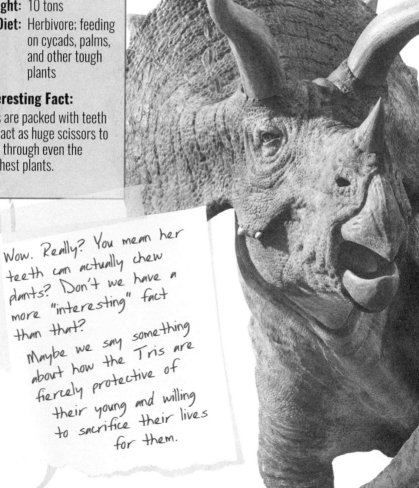

Wow. Really? You mean her teeth can actually chew plants? Don't we have a more "interesting" fact than that?

Maybe we say something about how the Tris are fiercely protective of their young and willing to sacrifice their lives for them.

This unique-looking creature has three horns and a frilled neck to protect her against larger dinosaurs like the *Carnotaurus*. *Triceratops* is not nearly as ferocious as a meat-eating dinosaur but is not harmless, either—she often locks horns in combat with her own species. This asset travels in herds and eats plants. Her name means "three-horned face."

A *Baby Triceratops* is the size of a softball when hatched and has a brain as small as a hazelnut. But she can grow to weigh 10 tons. While she's young, her horns are straight and extend only about 1 in. But, as you'll soon see, they don't stay small for long!

BARYONYX

Pronounced: *barr-ee-on-icks*

This amphibious asset walks on land and swims in water. She lurks on riverbanks ready to trap fish and other wriggling prey in her conical teeth. *Baryonyx* is a devious creature that communicates by clapping her jaws and thrashing in the water—just like her relative, the crocodile.

STATS

Length: 30.5 ft.
Weight: 2 tons
Diet: Carnivore; small to medium prey such as fish and baby dinosaurs

Interesting Fact:
Ancestors of this biped lurked in river deltas in Europe.

STEGOSAURUS

Pronounced: *steg-oh-sawr-us*

You might recognize this familiar-looking dinosaur by the 17 broad, bony plates set in two rows along her back. These plates make a *Stegosaurus* look bigger and scarier than she is. But this asset has a brain the size of walnut. She's a loner and very grumpy, so you don't want to be around when she swings her spiked tail at 120 ft. per second. Despite the massive size of this asset, *Stegosaurus* has tiny teeth, which limits her diet to soft plants. Her name means "roofed lizard."

STATS

Length: 33 ft.
Weight: 3.9 tons
Diet: Herbivore; soft, low-lying ferns and cycads

Interesting Fact:
Its tail has four spikes and is called a *thagomizer*.

A "thagomizer"? I did not know that. Guess you learn something new every day

ANKYLOSAURUS

Pronounced: *an-ky-low-sawr-us*

Often referred to as a "living tank," this creature's spiky scales—*osteoderms*—run the length of her body. She looks scary, but her scales are just for protection. *Ankylosaurus* is not terribly aggressive; she only eats plants—but a lot of them. Up to 130 pounds a day!

Make sure you always approach her from the front. Surprising her from behind could end you up on the bad end of that club too. Unless you like steel plates in your head or something...

STATS

Length: 33 ft.
Weight: 3.9 tons
Diet: Herbivore; soft, low-lying ferns and cycads

Interesting Fact:
This asset is so well-protected, even her eyelids have armor!

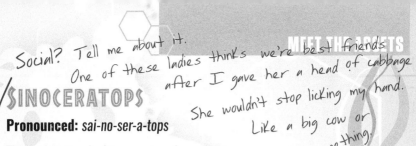

Social? Tell me about it. One of these ladies thinks we're best friends after I gave her a head of cabbage. She wouldn't stop licking my hand. Like a big cow or something.

SINOCERATOPS

Pronounced: *sai-no-ser-a-tops*

This interesting-looking creature has strong teeth to help her chew tough plants. Her skull has massive, flattened projections called *bosses*. One large boss looms over her nose and a smaller one over her eyes. This asset is very social and likes to live in large herds.

STATS

Length: 20 ft.
Weight: 3 tons
Diet: Herbivore; cycads and marsh plants

Interesting Fact:
Though this asset is an herbivore, sometimes the young add meat and bone to their diet to help fuel fast-growing skeletons.

29

MOSASAURUS

Pronounced: *mo-sa-sawr-us*

This fearsome asset is not an actual dinosaur, but an immense aquatic reptile. Her deadly array of teeth allows her to catch turtles, fish, birds, and even smaller *Mosasaurs*. A second set of teeth on her upper jaw ensures prey cannot escape. The asset hunts near the surface of the water. She has four paddle-like limbs and a powerful tail that helps her glide through her tank. An insatiable predator, she has huge jaws that can open wide enough to swallow her prey whole—even great white sharks!

STATS

Length: 85 ft.
Weight: 32 tons
Diet: Carnivore; sharks, fish, turtles, shellfish

Interesting Fact:
Monitor lizards and komodo dragons are this asset's closest modern relatives.

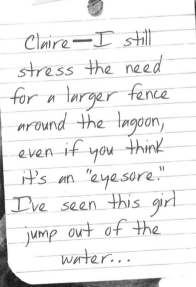

Claire—I still stress the need for a larger fence around the lagoon, even if you think it's an "eyesore." I've seen this girl jump out of the water...

PTERANODON

Pronounced: *terr-an-oh-don*

This flying predator has a 20 ft. wingspan and flies in squadron formation with others, presenting a terrifying front to prey. She's an aggressive, winged creature with no teeth. Instead, she uses a sharp, sword-like beak to snatch up her favorite food: fish. In fact, her name means "winged and toothless."

STATS

Length: 8.2 ft.
Weight: 6.6 lbs.
Diet: Carnivore; mostly fish

Interesting Fact:
The odd-looking point on this asset's head is called a *crest*. Males usually have more colorful crests than females.

TOP SECRET ASSET

Jurassic World adds a new attraction every few years to reinvigorate interest in the park and to add an additional "wow" factor to every visit. Anticipation for this TOP SECRET asset has been so high that guests have been pre-booking tickets months in advance. The asset is not yet available for public viewing, but we *can* say the Hammond Creation Lab has taken dinosaur genetic research to new heights, developing a creature the likes of which the world has never seen. *Spoiler alert*—this animal is even bigger than expected! As a Jurassic World employee, you will have the privilege of being among the first to see our magnificent new dinosaur.

If this doesn't get new employees excited about working here nothing will, don't you think?

—C

EXCITED? About working for a company that plays God for profit? This whole thing smells bad. Whatever you and Masrani are cooking up in that lab, make sure you put the safety of people and dinosaurs ahead of the almighty dollar.

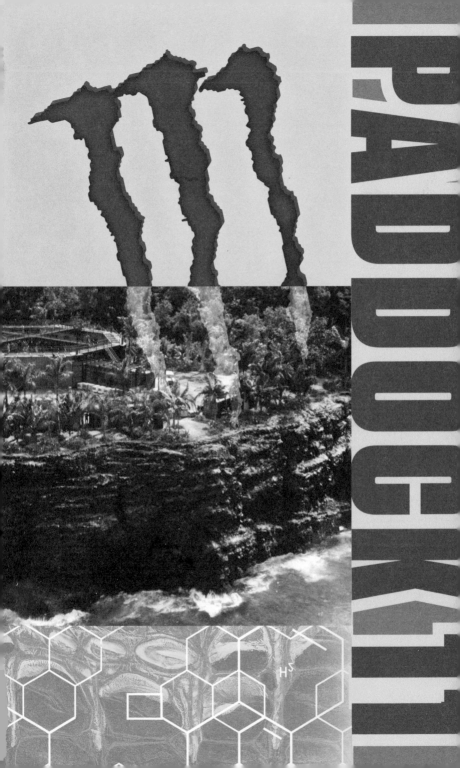

PADDOCK 11 STATS:

CAPACITY:	2 assets
CURRENT # OF ASSETS:	1
MILES FROM NEAREST ATTRACTION:	4
WALLS:	40 ft. tall (under construction to go higher)
MATERIAL:	Cement, reinforced with steel beams
DOORS:	Solid steel
FEEDING SYSTEM:	Crane
ASSET TRACKING:	Thermal detection system
SECURITY:	Handprint verification/ authorized personnel only

CEMENT FORTRESS

PADDOCK 11 is a cement fortress that currently houses our new TOP SECRET asset. The facility was designed by the finest structural engineers and is regularly evaluated for vulnerabilities. This paddock was built to guarantee the safety of the assets and our handlers.

SIZE UP?

Triceratops
& Baby Triceratops

Carnotaurus

Pteranodon

Sinoceratops

Ankylosaurus

HOW DO

Top Secret
Asset

Mosasaurus

THE DINOSAURS SIZE UP?

HOW DO THE DINOSAURS

Stygimoloch
(Stiggy)

Velociraptor

Tyrannosaurus Rex
(T. rex)

MAKING IT WORK

Jurassic World visitors expect perfection. It's our job to deliver it. Do you know what it takes to run a theme park? A lot more than you'd imagine. Below is a sampling of jobs most people never think of when they imagine careers in Jurassic World Theme Park and Resort.

Claire,

I know you've done a lot of different jobs in the park. Ever shovel out the paddocks? Because I'd pay money to have seen that. I'm lucky, InGen snapped me up right out of the Navy. No pun intended! :)

SHARK BAIT OPERATOR

Ever wonder who works behind the scenes of our most popular attractions? For example, who at Mosasaurus Stadium hoists the Great White shark onto the hook then glides it out over the lagoon? That would be the Shark Bait Operator. The job is not just getting the massive shark onto the hook, it means operating the pulley system and being precise. If the bait is too high, the asset misses. Too low, audiences leave without the huge splash they've come to expect. And feedings have to be executed perfectly every two hours, six shows a day, 7 days a week.

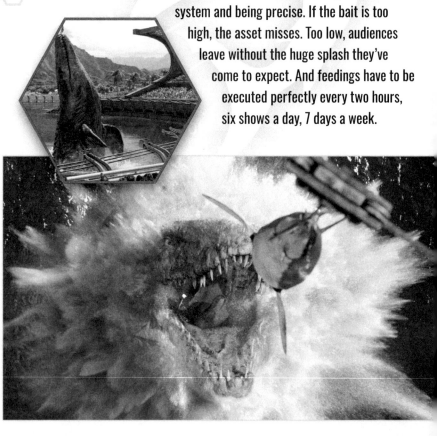

PETTING ZOO ATTENDANT

This is the perfect job for anyone who adores children and baby dinosaurs. Yet, as fun as the job can be, it's the attendant's responsibility to ensure the safety of our littlest visitors and their parents. After all, some of our sweetest dinosaurs weigh in at 800 lbs. and can do some damage if not properly supervised. It's also the attendant's job to arrive before visitors line up to make sure all assets are well fed, groomed, and calm. Once it's time to open the gate, this employee helps kids play with, ride, and even cuddle the young animals in safety.

BABY
TRICERATOPS
· JURASSIC WORLD ·
-PETTING ZOO-

Asset Containment Unit (ACU) Personnel

This position is part commando, part hunter. Most of our ACU security personnel are ex-military tactical specialists trained to track, capture, and use non-lethal force to neutralize assets and safely return them to their sectors or paddocks. ACU security personnel may only use lethal weapons if an asset is *a clear and present danger.*

Hotel Concierge

Yes, visitors flock to Jurassic World to hear our dinosaurs roar, but they also come to enjoy a relaxing vacation at the luxurious Isla Nublar Resort. The Concierge's job is to ensure guests receive great service. That might mean handing out maps, replacing lost room keys, hunting down missing luggage, or handling dinner, spa, or golf reservations for celebrities and other VIP guests. This is a job that requires resourcefulness, communication, and great people skills.

FOOD CART VENDOR

Whether selling hotdogs or handing out frozen lemonade, our Cart Vendors are friendly merchants who help our visitors grab a fast bite or refreshment so they can quickly move on to the next attraction. We consider cart vendors our remote ambassadors positioned throughout the park to offer directions, answer questions, or report problems. The job is ideal for an outgoing, friendly person who doesn't mind standing outdoors all day, sometimes in hot or rainy weather.

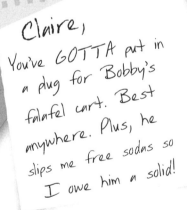

Claire,
You've GOTTA put in a plug for Bobby's falafel cart. Best anywhere. Plus, he slips me free sodas so I owe him a solid!

GYROSPHERE MECHANIC

This worker is a mechanical engineer skilled in gyroscopic technology. The job is to inspect every pod to make sure it is in perfect working order. That means balancing the gyroscope, checking for cracks, and making sure the joystick is oiled. The last thing we need is our guests stranded in a valley full of dinosaurs!

River Kayak Guide

This is a job for an outdoorsperson with excellent leadership skills. A guide must be familiar with our plant life and assets, with a focus on dinosaurs that hunt and forage in or around the river. Kayaking skills are a must as is certification in lifesaving and CPR. Most of our River Guides have degrees in one or more of the natural sciences.

FINISH

START

FERRY CAPTAIN

The job of Ferry Captain is shuttling visitors safely to and from the mainland in Costa Rica to our Ferry Landing on Isla Nublar. Ferries must run on time. On most trips, the seas are calm, but these pontoon-style vessels move through open seas and sometimes encounter bad weather and rough conditions. The Ferry Captain oversees a full crew, and is responsible for all safety protocols and drills. Ferries must be available at a moment's notice to be used for emergencies and evacuations. Most of our Ferry Captains are ex-Navy.

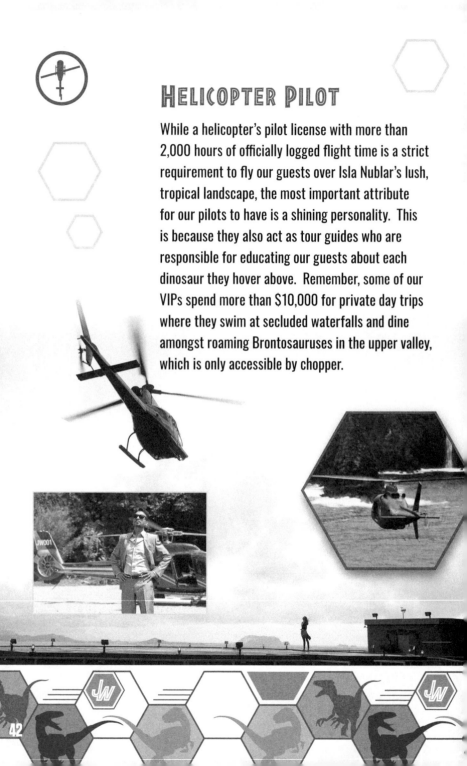

HELICOPTER PILOT

While a helicopter's pilot license with more than 2,000 hours of officially logged flight time is a strict requirement to fly our guests over Isla Nublar's lush, tropical landscape, the most important attribute for our pilots to have is a shining personality. This is because they also act as tour guides who are responsible for educating our guests about each dinosaur they hover above. Remember, some of our VIPs spend more than $10,000 for private day trips where they swim at secluded waterfalls and dine amongst roaming Brontosauruses in the upper valley, which is only accessible by chopper.

GYROSPHERE OPERATOR

There's more to this position than making sure people don't cut in line as they wait for their chance to travel around Gyrosphere Valley, although that is important. The Gyrosphere Operator's key responsibility is to ensure the safe and efficient loading and unloading of park guests from the vehicles. With so many people visiting Jurassic World each day, it is imperative that wait times be kept to a minimum, lest we begin to be compared to other theme parks.

PALEOVETERINARIAN

This is an animal doctor who specializes in dinosaurs. There are only a handful of these specialists, and they all work at Jurassic World. Their job entails everything from preventative care—vaccinations and parasite control—to treating assets for claw marks and bite wounds. On occasion, these doctors even perform surgery in the field. Sadly, some genetic anomalies arise from the cloning process and result in serious health problems for our assets. Our paleoveterinarians are trained to recognize and treat these rare genetic illnesses.

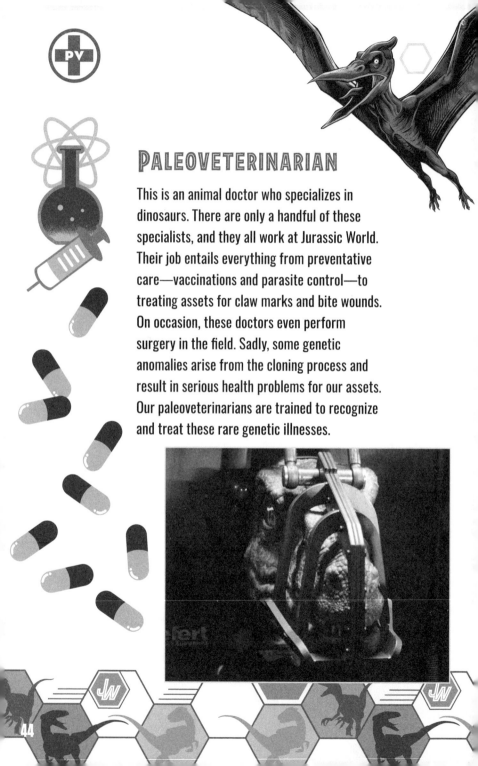

SENIOR BOTANIST

This is a crucial job that comes with enormous responsibilities. It means dispatching and supervising botany teams for each sector, monitoring the island's plant biodiversity, and educating the public. This is a scientist who knows paleobotany, ecology, genetics, and much more. A Senior Botanist ensures our herbivores remain in sectors where they can graze safely on the right plants. For example, years ago, a *Triceratops* fell ill after mistaking West Indian lilac berries for small stones that dinosaurs often swallow to help with digestion. The berries were poisonous and the *Triceratops* fell ill.

SHOPKEEPER/SOUVENIR SALES

It might not seem obvious, but a friendly, helpful shopkeeper plays a key role in the feeding and care of our assets, maintenance of our attractions, and furthering our genetic research. How is that possible? Well, admission ticket sales alone are not enough to cover the cost of running a massive theme park like Jurassic World. Souvenir revenue represents a healthy percentage of the park's income. Additionally, the T-shirt, hat, jacket, or keychain this employee sells will not only remind a visitor of their visit to Jurassic World for years to come, it might encourage a return visit.

BRACELET SCANBAND DISTRIBUTOR

This worker is among the first employees a guest meets upon arrival on Isla Nublar. When a visitor receives a ScanBand, he or she is getting a passport to the Theme Park, resort, and all of our retail establishments. The distributor's role is to inform guests about all the ScanBand's uses: it's a pass to enter attractions, a room key, and even acts as a debit card that links directly to their bank.

SANITATION WORKER

Jurassic World has its own advanced recycling system that processes 24,000 tons of cans, paper cardboard, plastic, and food waste every year. A sanitation worker is a vital part of this important operation. Sanitation isn't glamorous work, but it is as important as any job on the island. Without this service, bathrooms would go uncleaned, trashcans would overflow, and our assets' paddocks and tanks would become unlivable.

Okay, you finally got to it. But I still think you should just call it what it is: POOP REMOVAL. And by the way, you should stress that these guys are the real heroes on this island.

FLOWCHART

This flowchart does not include all the hundreds of employees who make Jurassic World operate seamlessly. It is merely a representation of the company's management structure, meant to show you what goes into operating the Theme Park, Resort, and Laboratory.

THE MASRANI GLOBAL CORPORATION

JURASSIC WORLD

 RESORT
(see no. 1 below)

 THEME PARK
(see no. 2 below)

 CREATION LAB
(see no. 3 below)

RESORT

HOTEL

Hospitality Manager

Concierge

Valet

Bellhop

Housekeeper

Pool Attendant

GOLF COURSE

Greenskeeper

Caddy

Golf Pro

Pro Shop Sales

Driving Range Attendant

SPA

Front Desk Clerk

Massage Therapist

Manicurist

Yoga Teacher

Skin Care Professional

WHAT IS EXPECTED OF YOU

E very employee at Jurassic World reflects the ethics
and integrity of all of us who work here. We insist on
high standards because we want our guests to trust us and
know we will always behave with integrity. This section
spells out how Jurassic World employees are expected to
conduct themselves at all times.

091TA7 87PP C87E C897R9N C05VEN 0U00 XOXO56470XO
000B71 R88 A> B 97FA 988 0000023III!////

STANDARDS OF CONDUCT

Whether your job is in the Theme Park, Resort, or Lab, we expect employees to act professionally at all times. This means being friendly and helpful to guests, respectful to superiors and co-workers, and performing your job well. We also expect you to be punctual, to treat park equipment and property with care, and to refrain from cursing, violence, or the use of alcohol or drugs. There is no smoking

I want to be as thorough as possible here because, of course, Jurassic World has unique safety issues. We have to meet standards that are much higher than your average theme park.

—C

allowed anywhere on the island. Personal smartphone use and social media are prohibited during work hours.

NOTE: *Improper conduct may result in verbal and/or written warnings, probation, or even termination.*

Claire,
I agree, you can't remind them enough that the safety of our visitors, employees, and assets is job #1. Dinosaurs may be cool, but no one should EVER forget they are dangerous animals to be aware of at all times. In fact, my mantra is: "Never turn your back to the cage."

DRESS CODE

All employees are expected to maintain a neat appearance. That means clothes are fresh, clean, and pressed. Your manager will provide you with the dress code for your area. In most cases that means a park-issued uniform. Below are a few examples of jobs and the uniforms they require:

- **ATTRACTION OPERATOR:** Brown shirt, brown pants, and matching cap with Jurassic World emblem.

- **LAB TECHNICIAN:** Gray lab coat with business attire underneath. Safety goggles, latex gloves, and close-toed lab shoes.

- **PARK RANGER:** Tan shirt with Jurassic World patch on the shoulder, blue pants, comfortable walking shoes.

- **PETTING ZOO ATTENDANT:** Khaki shirt with the park emblem, matching pants or shorts, and wide brimmed safari hat.

- **ACU PERSONNEL:** Gray shirt and pants, military-grade boots, and full tactical gear when engaged on a mission.

- **PADDOCK TECHNICIANS:** Blue coveralls, hard hat.

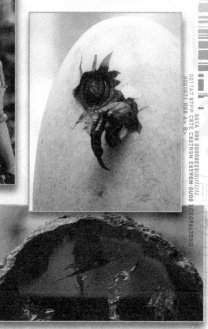

EXPERTISE

Jurassic World hires world-class scientists, skilled laborers, and workers that have been vetted in a highly-competitive interview and testing process. Every employee is expected to be an expert in his or her area.

NOTE:

Employees are encouraged to expand their expertise through our continuing education program taught by senior park employees. You can read about our class offerings in Section 8: Education and Career Advancement.

BACKGROUND CHECKS

Jurassic World employees are subject to regular, in-depth background checks. This ensures the highest integrity among our staff and guarantees both guests and employees are safe. Crime is nearly non-existent on Isla Nublar thanks to our top-notch security staff!

I want to use your photo here. Do I have your approval?

—C

Not my movie star side, but fine by me.

TERMINATION

Employees who fail to meet the standards of behavior set forth above are subject to termination. In most cases, an effort to address issues that led to the termination will take place before dismissal and include a probationary period, but that is not always possible.

Human Resources will assist with exit paperwork. Terminated employees have 24 hours to collect their belongings and depart the island. Security personnel will escort them to the ferry. Transportation to a country of origin is at the employee's expense.

All employees are required to read and sign a Confidentiality Agreement found at the end of Section 6.

TAKING CARE OF OUR OWN

At Jurassic World, we believe taking care of our employees makes for a happy, healthy work environment. In addition to our generous benefits package, we offer our staff nutritious food, comfortable accommodations, and some great perks.

MEALS

Our employee cafeteria serves a wide variety of healthy, balanced meals seven days a week. Cafeteria hours are 7 a.m. to 8 p.m. Employees can also use their IDs to receive discounts at park restaurants and shops when they are off-duty. We want workers to become familiar with all of our retail offerings so they can recommend them to our guests. At the end of this section, you can find a list of where you can use your employee discount for food (and merchandise) throughout the park.

**HERE'S A SAMPLE OF
WEEKLY SPECIALS SERVED
IN THE EMPLOYEE CAFETERIA.***

Sun:	Brunchasaurus
Mon:	Tuskcany baked lasagna
Tues:	*T. rex*-style Tacos
Weds:	Mammoth-sized Meatloaf
Thurs:	Eggs-tinct Benedict
Fri:	*Triceratops* Turkey Tetrazzini
Sat:	Pan-fried Prey of the Day

* Vegetarian entrees provided for herbivores.

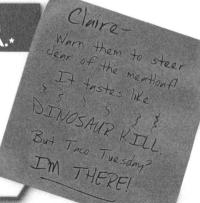

Claire—
Warn them to steer clear of the meatloaf! It tastes like DINOSAUR KILL. But Taco Tuesday? I'M THERE!

FUN EXTRAS

In addition to employee discounts for food and souvenirs, Jurassic World offers our employees *unlimited, free admission* to all attractions on days off. (Except on holidays or holiday weekends.).

EMPLOYEE ACCOMMODATIONS

Jurassic World, unlike other theme parks, is located miles from civilization on remote Isla Nublar. That's why we provide housing for all our employees in Jurassic Village. These accommodations are free and available based on job level and seniority. Employees are expected to keep their living quarters neat and clean. *Housekeeping services are available for an additional fee.*

Dormitories:	These are for interns and younger staff members
Private Dorm Rooms:	Suitable for many of our visiting scholars
Apartments:	Full apartments are available for employees with children
Townhouses:	For senior staff and available for other employees on a lottery basis
Hotel Rooms:	Jurassic World sets aside blocks of hotel rooms to house temporary and part-time employees who come to work on the island during peak season

VACATION AND FURLOUGH DAYS

Jurassic World Employees accrue vacation time and are eligible for pre-approved furlough days during which they can visit the mainland. Jurassic World works in partnership with many resorts in Costa Rica that offer our employees discounts on accommodations, activities, and food.

NOTE:

Our ferries are the only mode of transportation to the island. Space is at a premium and they fill up fast. Therefore, you must book your return ferry ride to Isla Nublar in advance and return as *scheduled*.

Owen,

Too many employees abuse the ferry policy. I'm thinking of adding: "If you miss your boat you will lose your job— no ifs, ands, or buts." What do you think?

—C

Harsh much?
   Even baseball players get three strikes.

HEALTH BENEFITS

Full-time employees at Jurassic World receive full health care coverage through the Masrani Healthcare Network. This includes access to the island's state-of-the-art medical facility and its staff of highly-skilled health care workers. Our doctors are specifically trained to treat dinosaur bites and scratches, and to diagnose and treat modern and prehistoric diseases.

JURASSIC WORLD WILL COVER THE COST OF THESE REQUIRED IMMUNIZATIONS:

HEPATITIS A	POLIO
HEPATITIS B	TDAP
TYPHOID	MMR
YELLOW FEVER	VARICELLA
MALARIA	PNEUMONIA
DIPHTHERIA	ROTAVIRUS
MENINGITIS	ZIKA VIRUS
TYPHOID FEVER	RABIES
	(for dinosaur bites and scratches)

SICK LEAVE

Jurassic World employees get 8 paid sick days per year. Senior employees get 11. Sick leave is typically used for preventative care, doctor appointments, and/or recovery from an illness or injury. We highly encourage employees with cold or flu symptoms to use their sick days. Up to 30,000 visitors circulate through the park each day. We want them to take home our souvenirs not our germs!

STRESS REDUCTION PROGRAM

At Jurassic World, we believe a healthy mind leads to a healthy life. Let's face it, even the greatest job in a beautiful place like Isla Nublar has its stressors—just talk to some of our dinosaur handlers! That's why we encourage all of our employees to participate in our full range of stress reduction activities:

OUR PROGRAM INCLUDES:

Yoga Classes	Bicycling
Nutrition Classes	Sailing
Tai Chi	Paddleboarding
Walking and Running Groups	Meditation

And just for fun, at the end of this section you'll find a few pages from our top-selling adult coloring book (available in our gift shops). Studies show coloring slows the heart rate and lowers blood pressure. So enjoy and relax!

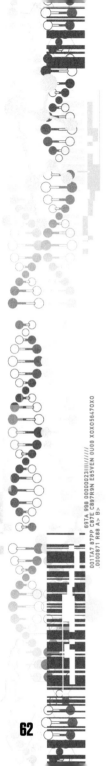

CONFIDENTIALITY

Jurassic World Theme Park, Resort, and the Hammond Creation Lab operate at the cutting edge of genetic engineering, ecological innovation, hospitality, and entertainment development. As an employee you are expected to keep confidential all data that is not available to the public. This includes, but is not limited to, information about asset development, scientific research, attraction information, hotel promotions, and marketing. This discretion applies to verbal, written, printed, and electronic materials. Your dedication to confidentiality protects our company from the theft of ideas and materials, and ensures the future of Jurassic World in a competitive market.

On P. 64, you will find an Employee Confidentiality Agreement. Please read it, sign, and date it. Then return the document to your supervisor at your upcoming orientation.

001TA7 87PP C87E C897RON E65VEN
.000B71 R88 A> B>

69TA 998 000000023

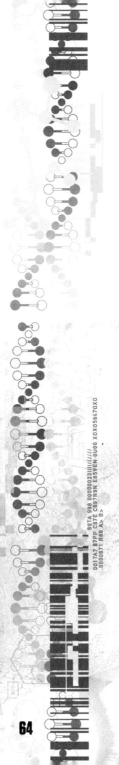

CONFIDENTIALITY AGREEMENT

As an employee of Jurassic World, I confirm that I will keep all forms of information listed below about Jurassic World Theme Park, Jurassic World Resort, and/or The Hammond Creation Lab strictly confidential.

This Confidential Information includes:

Research, inventions, technical and business information, patented ideas, trade secrets, drawings, illustrations, models, emails, asset development information, attraction development information, marketing, and financial data.

I acknowledge that I have read and understand this Agreement and voluntarily accept all duties and obligations set forth herein.

_____

Print Employee Name

_____ / /

Employee Signature   *Date*

Coloring For Fun And Relaxation

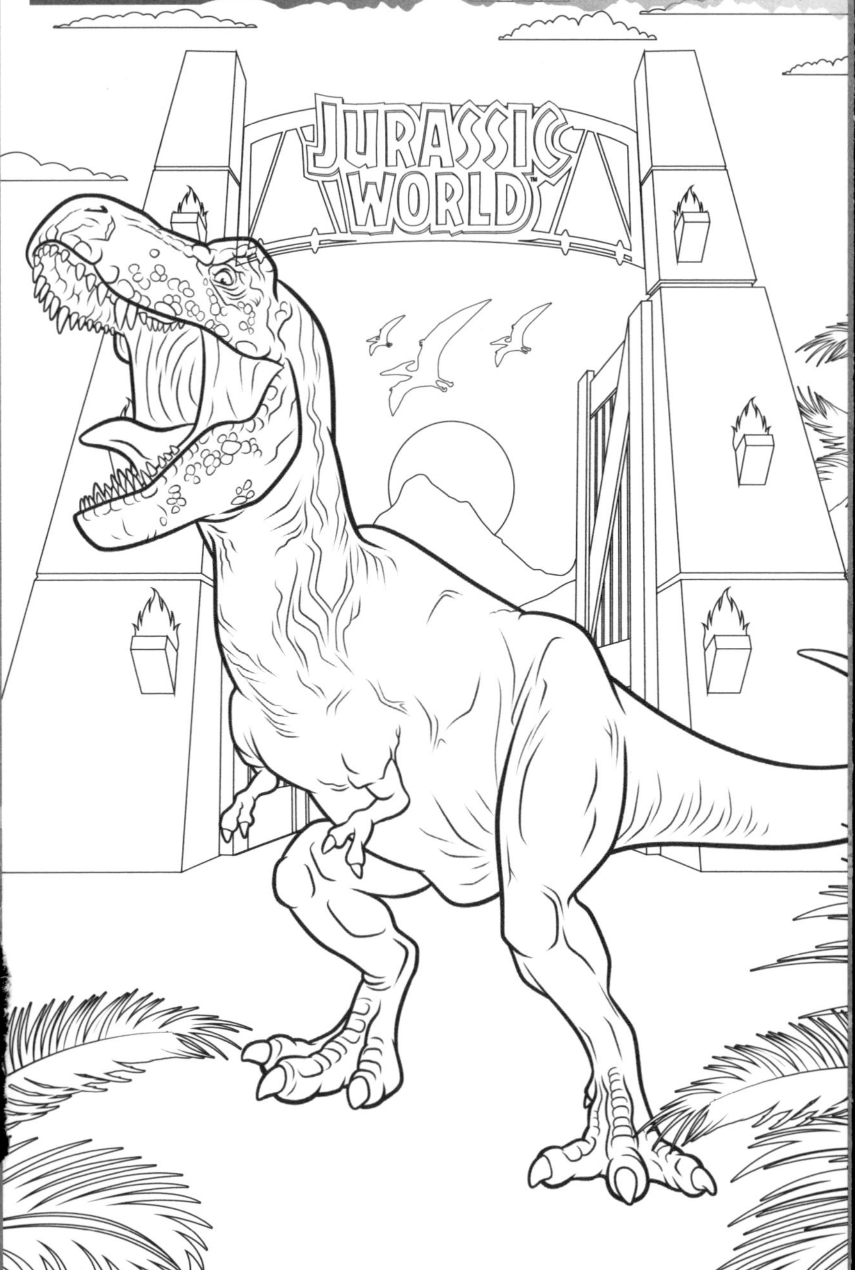

FOOD

Baked by Melissa
Ben & Jerry's
Bobby's Falafel Stand
Dave & Busters
Margaritaville
Mike & Ike Candy
Nobu
Starbucks
Sunrio
Jamba Juice
Winston Steakhouse!
Yoshinoya

SHOPS

Brookstone
Caliza Spa
Columbia
Havaianas
IWC
Jurassic Traders
Oakley

EMPLOYEE DISCOUNTS

EMPLOYEE DISCOUNTS

Use your employee ID to get 30% off at all our great Jurassic World eateries and shops. Here are some park favorites:

WORK SAFE, WORK SMART

As you've learned by now, safety is our top priority. Jurassic World is a self-contained city with its own security, medical, safety, and firefighting personnel. A team of trained operations, safety, and security experts oversees our high-tech safety network. Nevertheless, *every* Jurassic World employee is expected to take part in ensuring the safety and well-being of our guests. This is why it is important that you read this section carefully.

CONTROL CENTER

Our Control Center is equipped with the best technology available. Here we are able to track all visitors and employees, and oversee Theme Park, Resort, and Lab security. Some areas in the park are accessible only by thumb or handprint scan. We also have an **advanced asset tracking system** that relies on implants to let us know where assets

are at all times. Our goal is a 100% safety record. To achieve this, we prepare our employees for everything from routine incidents, like a lost child or a guest with heatstroke, to the unthinkable—a **Code 19: Asset Escape!**

Owen, definitely give this a thorough read. I want input from someone with hands-on experience. Security and legal are reviewing it next.

—C

Stress that employees — especially new hires— should always be on guard. They MUST take their security training seriously and never forget many of these dinosaurs are KILLING MACHINES — it's in their nature. One must respect this about them. Fear is healthy here. A good time to repeat my mantra: "Never turn your back to the cage!"

ROUTINE INCIDENTS

Operating a theme park and resort means knowing some incidents come with the territory. Our first line of defense is prevention. When this fails, security personnel are on patrol throughout the park to intervene. They are trained in hazard detection, first aid, and CPR. Some are certified as EMTs. If you are aware of or suspect any of the problems listed below please do not attempt to handle them yourself; call Security immediately.

DEHYDRATION

SUNBURN

SUNSTROKE

DRUNKENNESS

THEFT

VANDALISM

DISORDERLY CONDUCT

BULLYING

LOST CHILDREN

POWER OUTAGES

LIGHTNING STRIKES

INJURIES

HEART ATTACKS

ASSET HARASSMENT

GYROSPHERE SAFETY

Our Gyrosphere safety record is nearly perfect. Mechanical breakdowns are rare. That's because each pod is equipped with safety features that prevent incidents before they occur. Each pod is outfitted with:

GYROSCOPIC TECHNOLOGY:	keeps the pod upright at all times.
SEATBELTS:	fully reinforced, to protect guests in the extremely unlikely event of a collision or rollover.
BULLETPROOF GLASS:	made from aluminum oxynitride, strong enough to stop a .50 caliber bullet.
ROLLAWAY SYSTEM:	automatically rolls the pod a safe distance from an asset if it gets too close.
TRACKING:	every pod is equipped with a tracker that is monitored from our Control Center.
INVISIBLE BARRIER SYSTEM:	keeps pods and assets within designated areas.

LABORATORY SAFETY

All lab workers receive a Hammond Creation Lab Safety Manual along with this Handbook. These are both required reading. The Manual defines lab protocols and procedures, covering everything from protective gear and incubator maintenance to contagious dinosaur infections. A partial list of protocols covered in your lab Safety Manual is below:

PERSONAL SAFETY

EQUIPMENT SAFETY

CHEMICAL AND GAS SAFETY

FIRE SAFETY

DISINFECTION AND STERILIZATION

ASSET HANDLING

HAZARDOUS BIOLOGICAL MATERIALS

LABORATORY-ACQUIRED INFECTIONS

EMERGENCY PROCEDURES

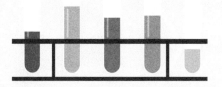

PADDOCK SAFETY AND CONTAINMENT BREACH

PADDOCK SAFETY

Our invisible fence technology keeps our more docile assets from roaming outside their designated zones. But lethal assets require a higher degree of security. That's why they are housed in cement and steel-reinforced paddocks miles from the nearest attraction. Our structural engineers designed these facilities with impenetrable walls that can withstand massive amounts of force. This ensures the safety of employees and visitors. It also protects the animals and preserves our investment in them. Asset development can cost millions for each creature!

ASSET BREACH

In the rare event an asset escapes, employees will receive a text and/or hear an announcement stating: "Code 19." This will trigger an emergency response from the Asset Containment Unit and security personnel. All of our assets are implanted with a tracking chip that monitors its vital signs and emits a beacon. The ACU also employs *thermal technology* to track, locate, and contain an asset quickly.

If for any reason an asset *cannot* be contained, the park will broadcast this announcement: "Ladies and Gentlemen, due to a containment anomaly, all guests must take shelter immediately." This will initiate our Phase I protocol, meaning all attractions should be shut down and safety captains must report to Security to assist with evacuations. Everyone north of the resort must be moved into designated shelters.

ACU may only use live ammunition in the event an asset cannot be contained and poses a *clear and present danger.*

EARTHQUAKE OR VOLCANIC ERUPTION

Among the dangers on Isla Nublar are earthquakes, which are common in the region. A volcanic eruption is less likely, but we need to be prepared for either. In the event of natural disasters like these, Jurassic World has backup power generators, food lockers, first aid trailers, and everything needed for employees and visitors to shelter in place for up to a week. First responders and medical personnel live and work on the island, so they are close by and available to administer first aid.

EARTHQUAKE

In the event of an earthquake, all attractions are to be shut down immediately and guests must be escorted to designated safe zones. Safety teams will go through the park to assess damage. If they determine it is safe to resume regular operations, things proceed as normal. If not, the island will be evacuated using safety protocols outlined in each department's Safety Manual.

VOLCANIC ERUPTION

Isla Nublar formed when an underwater volcano spewed molten rock onto the sea floor and built up above sea level. Volcanoes like ours are considered "active" if they have erupted in the past 10,000 years. An erupting volcano can blast ash, lava, solid rocks, and gases into the air, creating hazards that can kill, disrupt air travel, and destroy property. In the highly-unlikely event of a volcanic eruption, attractions will shut down, and employees and security personnel will direct guests to designated shelters stocked with supplies for up to one week. Shelters are also stocked with face masks and eye goggles. Everyone is to put them on. Make sure all windows are closed. Avoid areas downwind of the volcano, river valleys downstream of the volcano, and all low-lying areas. Debris and ash will be carried by wind and gravity. Keep windows shut and limit any movement to areas where you will not be further exposed to volcanic hazards.

I can already hear what you're thinking. Volcano?

—C

YES, Volcano! Who was the whiz kid that decided to build this place on what basically amounts to a ticking time bomb floating in the middle of the ocean?

CAREER ADVANCEMENT/ EDUCATIONAL DEVELOPMENT

At Jurassic World, we believe advancing our employees' careers is an investment in all of our futures. That's why we offer equal opportunity promotions and educational opportunities for all our workers. We want our team members to bring enthusiasm to the job, and we regularly promote workers who are eager to set and attain professional goals. Yes, even a food server can aspire to become a research specialist working face-to-face with the dinosaurs!

The following section is a sampling of course offerings at Jurassic World. A full course catalog will be available at your orientation.

COURSE NAME: DINOSAUR SURVIVAL

INSTRUCTOR: *Owen Grady, Dinosaur Behaviorist*

COURSE DESCRIPTION:

In this hands-on workshop, Dinosaur Behaviorist Owen Grady takes you into the field to demonstrate safety protocols. The class begins with Grady's mantra: "Never turn your back to the cage" and ends with participants working hands-on with some of our moderately aggressive assets.

I gave you your class. Happy?

Glad you listened. But you forgot to mention my boyish charm and rugged good looks....

LEADERSHIP DEVELOPMENT INTENSIVE

INSTRUCTOR *Claire Dearing, Operations Manager**

COURSE DESCRIPTION:

This is an afternoon survey on leadership development skills. Topics covered include: High-Impact Leadership, Criticism and Discipline Skills for Managers, Developing and Supervising High Performing Teams, Public Speaking, Basic Presentation Skills, and Measuring Presentation Impact.

*Time permitting

This is awesome, Claire!
But why just an afternoon?
I'm sure you've got enough
business smarts to fill up
an entire semester.

Systems Administration

INSTRUCTORS: *Lowery Cruthers & Vivian Krill, Control Room Systems Analyst*

COURSE DESCRIPTION:

Systems Analysts Lowery Cruthers and Vivian Krill describe the intricate systems that keep Jurassic World operating smoothly. This includes a rare visit to the Control Room with demonstrations of asset tracking, personnel monitoring, and our invisible fence technology!

SECURITY ADMINISTRATION

INSTRUCTOR: *Vic Hoskins, Private Security Commander*

COURSE DESCRIPTION:

Commander Vic Hoskins describes the role a security force plays in any organization.

He lays out the hierarchy of command and dives into topics including: Operation Planning and Strategies, Cutting-Edge Security Technology, Background Checks, and Exploring Real-World Applications for Dinosaurs.

No. I don't like the idea of Vic teaching a class. We can talk more in person, but something about this guy gives me the willies...

The Entrepreneurial Spirit

INSTRUCTOR: *Simon Masrani, Owner and CEO,
Masrani Global Industries*

COURSE DESCRIPTION:

Corporate mogul and Renaissance man Simon Masrani offers employees a rare glimpse into his thought processes. In this hour-long lecture, he describes what it takes to run a multi-national conglomerate and explains how his commitment to innovation, creativity, and risk-taking have contributed to his success in industries as far reaching as oil, construction, and biogenetics.

Note: Mr. Masrani is a busy man whose class is only offered once a year—it fills up within hours of being announced. So act fast! Seating is limited to 300.

SAMPLE COURSE SIGNUP FORM

Employee Name

Department   Email

Course Selection

This form is on the Jurassic World website under Employee Opportunities: Educational Development. Please complete the form online and email it to your immediate supervisor.

A LETTER FROM DR. HENRY WU

Since childhood, I have been fascinated by science and man's ability to harness it for his own purposes. At Jurassic World, I am fortunate to have the opportunity and resources to shatter outdated scientific theory and lift biogenetic engineering and technology to levels that were unimaginable even a half-century ago. Today, I continue to push the boundaries of scientific exploration. I am making discoveries that will amaze even the greatest scientific minds!

As an employee of Jurassic World, you each play a role in bringing the fruits of my research to the public. In this section, I will guide you through a brief tutorial on genetics, the science that created the magnificent dinosaurs you see on Isla Nublar.

Dr. Henry Wu

Dr. Henry Wu

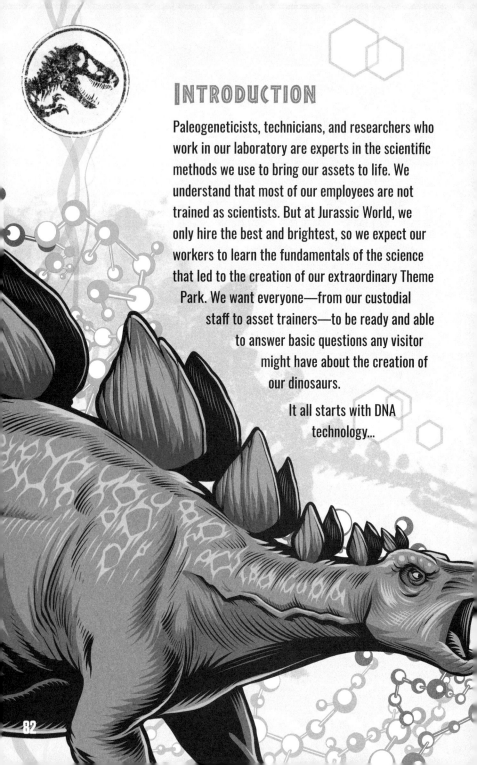

Introduction

Paleogeneticists, technicians, and researchers who work in our laboratory are experts in the scientific methods we use to bring our assets to life. We understand that most of our employees are not trained as scientists. But at Jurassic World, we only hire the best and brightest, so we expect our workers to learn the fundamentals of the science that led to the creation of our extraordinary Theme Park. We want everyone—from our custodial staff to asset trainers—to be ready and able to answer basic questions any visitor might have about the creation of our dinosaurs.

It all starts with DNA technology...

WHAT IS GENETIC SCIENCE?

Genetics is a biological science that studies inherited characteristics and their variations.

WHAT IS DNA?

DNA stands for deoxyribonucleic acid. This microscopic material is invisible to the naked eye but present in nearly all living things. In fact, one drop of blood contains billions of strands of DNA! Think of DNA as a blueprint for creating a living thing. That's why DNA is called "the building blocks of life." Some living things—like dinosaurs—went extinct millions of years ago. But because they left their DNA, or "blueprints," behind we can travel back through time, read them, and "rebuild" these creatures in a process called *cloning*.

WHAT ARE GENES?

Genes are made up of this DNA arranged in different orders. These patterns are "instructions" that tell organisms how to create proteins.

DINOSAUR GENETICS

Remember we compared DNA to a blueprint? And said a billion strands of DNA exist in one drop of blood? Well, dinosaur blood—or the DNA it contains—is the material we use to develop our assets.

Millions of years ago, dinosaurs were not the only creatures that lived on earth. There were mosquitos, too. And just like today, mosquitos stung other creatures to suck up their blood. Unfortunately for them—but fortunately for us—some of these insects got stuck in tree sap and died.

Over millions of years, the mosquitos and the sap became fossilized together. Fossilized tree sap is called *amber*. Our researchers discovered that these

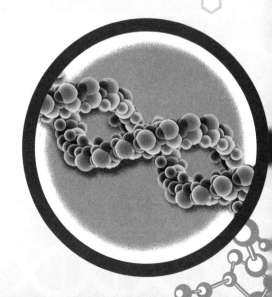

prehistoric mosquitos were genetic gold mines loaded with dinosaur DNA. In fact, just one strain of dinosaur DNA contains 3 billion genetic codes!

Once our scientists were able to extract the blood from these insects, they could read the DNA it contained. Today, the Hammond Creation Lab is equipped with the most current, high-tech gene sequencers in existence. Our instruments can read and break down DNA strands in minutes. Once we know the sequences of a dinosaur's DNA or its "blueprint," we can replicate it, and create baby dinosaurs!

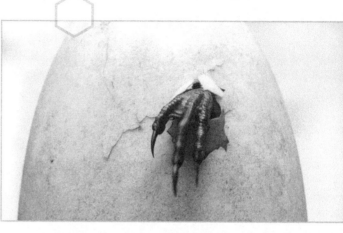

DINOSAUR BIOLOGY

Dinosaurs come from a group of reptiles called *archosauromorphs* and are most closely related to today's birds and lizards. Like reptiles and birds, dinosaurs lay eggs. But when we started cloning dinosaurs we did not have females to lay eggs. We had to create baby dinosaurs genetically through the process of cloning. In time, a few small cells turn into an embryo surrounded by a shell—a dinosaur egg. Here, in our lab, our baby dinosaurs are hatched, raised, and released into the Theme Park.

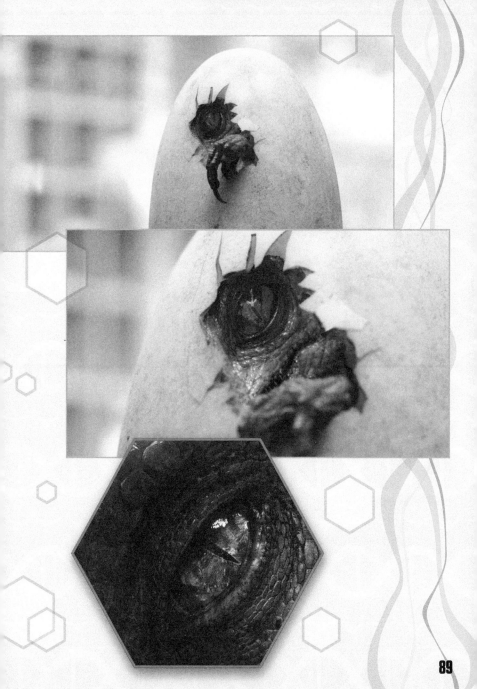

A TOUR OF THE LAB

The Hammond Creation Lab is the only facility of its kind in the entire world. Here we use our patented genetic engineering technology to clone dinosaurs that grow up to become the happy, healthy specimens you see on Isla Nublar.

The Lab is divided into five departments: *Extraction, Sequencing, Assembly, Hatchery*, and *Nursery*. Essentially, we have created a genetic assembly line to "build" dinosaurs.

Build? I really don't like the sound of that.

In our Extraction Department, technicians pull or *extract* the dinosaur DNA from fossilized amber that has been discovered all over the world. Next, the DNA goes to Sequencing where it is "read" with the help of a gene sequencer. Then one of our paleogeneticists in the Assembly department assembles the new genetic material into growing dinosaur cells, which are then sent to the Hatchery to be grown or incubated. Our Incubation Techs, Biodevice Engineers, and Asset Supervisors monitor the cells to ensure they continue to replicate properly and form a healthy dinosaur embryo encased in a shell.

If all goes well, a beautiful baby dinosaur will emerge from the egg to greet the world. Subsequently, she'll be transferred to our Nursery to be raised in the care of our Paleoveterinarians, Hatchery Supervisors, and Dinosaur Behaviorists. Baby dinosaurs stay in the Nursery until they are old enough to join the general population.

SPECIM

Two pictures of me
in one book?
I'm flattered!

92

OUR ASSETS'
FRAGILE ECO-SYSTEM

Dinosaurs went extinct because of a natural catastrophe. Now that human beings have brought these prehistoric creatures back to life, we do not want to be the cause of their undoing once again. Isla Nublar is 120 miles out at sea, but we share the planet with the modern world and its factories, freeways, and waste. We built Jurassic World on Isla Nublar, far from civilization, to give our assets a home as pristine as the habitat their ancestors roamed millions of years ago. But their eco-system is a fragile one. So we work hard to preserve this island's towering mountains and sweeping plains as their sanctuary.

Jurassic World was built to have as little impact on the island as possible. We recycle and use biodegradable materials. We monitor the water, soil, and air to make sure they are pure and clean. We urge our employees to respect this island and to teach our visitors to do the same. We hope you will always remember that you are not just employees of a theme park, you are teachers and emissaries to the outside world, here to preserve nature—and our assets —in all their historic wonder.

IN CLOSING: YOUR BRIGHT FUTURE

A career at Jurassic World is like no other on the planet. There's a lot to learn about working in this unique, sometimes dangerous, but always-thrilling environment. There is also a lot to learn about your new life as a resident of Isla Nublar. In fact, there is so much to take in it can feel overwhelming. That's why I encourage you to read the information contained in this Handbook again and again. It was written to make your learning curve a little less steep, to help you become a confident and productive member of our team. Use it as a handy reference when you find yourself in any circumstance that leaves you unsure or questioning your next move.

Finally, we are all eager to begin a long and fruitful working relationship with you. While our assets are taken from the past, our future is bright and limitless, and we are all delighted that you will be walking into that bright future with us.

Claire Dearing

Claire Dearing
Operations Manager

ALL EMPLOYEES MUST READ AND SIGN THIS EMPLOYEE ACKNOWLEDGEMENT FORM AND RETURN IT TO THEIR SUPERVISOR AT ORIENTATION.

EMPLOYEE ACKNOWLEDGEMENT

This Employee Handbook contains important information about the Jurassic World Theme Park, Jurassic World Resort, and the Hammond Creation Lab. I have had an opportunity to read the handbook and understand I may ask my supervisor any questions I might have about it. I accept the terms of the Handbook and understand it is my responsibility to comply with the policies contained in it.

I also understand that I am expected to read the entire handbook and that my signature below confirms my commitment to do so.

_____

_____
DATE

Claire,
Congrats on a job well done. I've added some comments throughout, but think that I give my best advice in person. Say, tomorrow night at Margaritaville—just you, me, and Jimmy Buffet!

Studio Fun International
An imprint of Printers Row Publishing Group
A division of Readerlink Distribution Services, LLC
10350 Barnes Canyon Road, Suite 100, San Diego, CA 92121
www.studiofun.com

Written by Gina Gold
Designed by Todd Taliaferro
Creative development by Judy O Productions, Inc.

Printers Row Publishing Group is a division of Readerlink Distribution Services, LLC.
Studio Fun International is a registered trademark of Readerlink Distribution Services, LLC.

All notations of errors or omissions should be addressed to Studio Fun International, Editorial Department, at the above address.

ISBN: 978-0-7944-4194-4
Manufactured, printed, and assembled in Stevens Point, WI, U.S.A.
First printing. April 2018, WOR/04/18
22 21 20 19 18 1 2 3 4 5